LOVE YOU FOREVER

WRITTEN BY ROBERT MUNSCH
ILLUSTRATED BY SHEILA McGRAW

FIREFLY BOOKS

A FIREFLY BOOK

Published by Firefly Books Ltd.
Text copyright © 1986 by Robert Munsch
Text copyright © 1987 by Bob Munsch Enterprises, Ltd.
Illustration copyright © Sheila McGraw Toronto Inc.

98th printing, 2015

Cataloguing in Publication Data

Munsch, Robert N., 1945-
Love you forever

ISBN-10: 0-920668-36-4 (bound). – ISBN-10: 0-920668-37-2 (pbk.)
ISBN-13: 978-0-920668-36-8 – ISBN-13: 978-0-920668-37-5

ISBN-10: 1-895565-66-9 (special slipcased edition)
ISBN-13: 978-1-895565-66-9

I. McGraw, Sheila. II. Title.

PS8576.U58L68 1986   jC8138.54   C86-094624-X
PZ7.M86Lo 1986

Published in Canada by
Firefly Books Ltd.
50 Staples Avenue, Unit 1
Richmond Hill, Ontario L4B 0A7

Published in the United States by
Firefly Books (U.S.) Inc.
P.O. Box 1338, Ellicott Station
Buffalo, New York, USA 14205

Design: Klaus Uhlig Designgroup Inc.

Printed in Canada

To
Ann Munsch
and
Andrew, Julie, Tyya, Sam, and Gilly Munsch,
and to my Mom and Dad,
Thomas John Munsch 1912-2005
Margaret McKeon Munsch 1914-2006

A mother held her new baby and
very slowly rocked him back and forth,
back and forth, back and forth.
And while she held him, she sang:

I'll love you forever,
I'll like you for always,
As long as I'm living
my baby you'll be.

The baby grew. He grew and he grew and he grew. He grew until he was two years old, and he ran all around the house. He pulled all the books off the shelves. He pulled all the food out of the refrigerator and he took his mother's watch and flushed it down the toilet. Sometimes his mother would say, *"This kid is driving me CRAZY!"*

But at night time, when that two-year-
old was quiet, she opened the door
to his room, crawled across the floor,
looked up over the side of his bed;
and if he was really asleep she picked
him up and rocked him back and forth,
back and forth, back and forth.
While she rocked him she sang:

> I'll love you forever,
> I'll like you for always,
> As long as I'm living
> my baby you'll be.

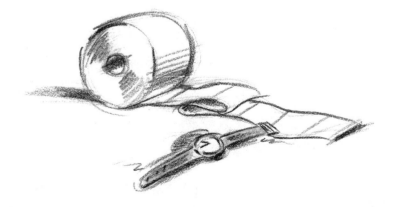

The little boy grew. He grew and he grew and he grew. He grew until he was nine years old. And he never wanted to come in for dinner, he never wanted to take a bath, and when grandma visited he always said bad words. Sometimes his mother wanted to sell him to the *zoo!*

But at night time, when he was
asleep, the mother quietly opened the
door to his room, crawled across
the floor and looked up over the side of
the bed. If he was really asleep,
she picked up that nine-year-old boy
and rocked him back and forth,
back and forth, back and forth.
And while she rocked him, she sang:

> I'll love you forever,
> I'll like you for always,
> As long as I'm living
> my baby you'll be.

The boy grew. He grew and he grew and he grew and he grew. He grew until he was a teenager. He had strange friends and he wore strange clothes and he listened to strange music. Sometimes his mother felt like she was in a *zoo!*

But at night time, when that teenager
was asleep, the mother opened the door
to his room, crawled across the
floor and looked up over the side
of the bed. If he really was asleep she
picked up that great big boy and rocked
him back and forth, back and forth,
back and forth.
While she rocked him she sang:

> I'll love you forever,
> I'll like you for always,
> As long as I'm living
> my baby you'll be.

That teenager grew. He grew and he grew and he grew and he grew. He grew until he was a grown-up man. He left home and got a house across town.

But sometimes on dark nights
the mother got into her car and drove
across town.

If all the lights in her son's house
were out, she opened his bedroom
window, crawled across the floor,
and looked up over the side of his bed.
If that great big man was really
asleep she picked him up and rocked
him back and forth, back and forth,
back and forth.
And while she rocked him she sang:

> I'll love you forever,
> I'll like you for always,
> As long as I'm living
> my baby you'll be.

Well, that mother, she got older.
She got older and older and older.
One day she called up her son and said,
"You'd better come see me because
I'm very old and sick."
So her son came to see her.
When he came in the door she tried
to sing the song. She sang:

> I'll love you forever,
> I'll like you for always…

But she couldn't finish because she
was too old and sick.

The son went to his mother.
He picked her up and rocked her
back and forth, back and forth,
back and forth.
And he sang this song:

>I'll love you forever,
>I'll like you for always,
>As long as I'm living
>my Mommy you'll be.

When the son came home
that night, he stood for a long time
at the top of the stairs.

Then he went into the room
where his very new baby daughter
was sleeping. He picked her up in
his arms and very slowly rocked
her back and forth, back and forth,
back and forth.
And while he rocked her he sang.

> I'll love you forever,
> I'll like you for always,
> As long as I'm living
> my baby you'll be.

Robert Munsch

Robert Munsch is one of North America's best-selling children's authors.
His books are staples of any child's library. All together they have sold
over 30 million copies, and have been translated into over a dozen languages.
Every year Munsch receives thousands of letters from young fans. He likes to meet
the children who send him mail, which sometimes leads to another story. Of his touring
schedule, he says simply, "I love it! One of the nicest things about my job is traveling across
North America and meeting all kinds of people." See www.robertmunsch.com.

Sheila McGraw

is an expat Canadian living in Texas. She is the mother of three grown sons.
McGraw is the author and illustrator of the books *Pussycats Everywhere!* and *Papier-Mâché
for Kids* (winner of the Benjamin Franklin Award) and *Painting and Decorating Furniture*.
Her art can be viewed at www.SheilaMcGraw.com.

Books by Sheila McGraw:
This Old New House • Papier-Mâché Today
Papier-Mâché For Kids • Soft Toys to Sew • Gifts Kids Can Make
I Promise I'll Find You (illustrator) • Dolls Kids Can Make
Painting and Decorating Furniture • Pussycats Everywhere

Books by Robert Munsch:
Something Good • Angela's Airplane • The Fire Station • Pigs
A Promise Is a Promise • Moira's Birthday • I Have to Go!
50 Below Zero • The Boy in the Drawer • Murmel Murmel Murmel
Mud Puddle • The Paper Bag Princess • Mortimer • Thomas' Snowsuit
David's Father • Jonathan Cleaned Up • Millicent and the Wind
The Dark • Where Is Gah-Ning? • Wait and See
Purple, Green and Yellow • Show and Tell • Stephanie's Ponytail
From Far Away (all published by Annick Press)